TIMELE〈

MW00523115

ROMEO AND JULIET

William Shakespeare

– ADAPTED BY –

Patricia Hutchison

SADDLEBACK
EDUCATIONAL PUBLISHING

TIMELESS SHAKESPEARE

Copyright ©2013 by Saddleback Educational Publishing

ISBN-13: 978-1-62250-712-2
eBook: 978-1-61247-963-7

Printed in Malaysia

23 22 21 20 19   4 5 6 7 8

— Contents —

	The Prologue	7
ACT 1	Scene 1	7
	Scene 2	16
	Scene 3	20
	Scene 4	23
	Scene 5	26
ACT 2	Scene 1	31
	Scene 2	33
	Scene 3	40
	Scene 4	43
	Scene 5	47
	Scene 6	49
ACT 3	Scene 1	51
	Scene 2	59
	Scene 3	63
	Scene 4	68
	Scene 5	70
ACT 4	Scene 1	76
	Scene 2	81
	Scene 3	84
	Scene 4	86
	Scene 5	88
ACT 5	Scene 1	91
	Scene 2	94
	Scene 3	96

— Cast of Characters —

Montague family and friends:

ROMEO MONTAGUE: A young man

LORD MONTAGUE: Romeo's father and the enemy of Lord Capulet

LADY MONTAGUE: Romeo's mother

MERCUTIO: Romeo's friend and Prince Escalus's cousin

BENVOLIO: Romeo's cousin and friend

BALTHASAR: Romeo's servant

ABRAHAM: Lord Montague's servant

FRIAR LAWRENCE: A Franciscan priest

FRIAR JOHN: Friar Lawrence's friend

— Cast of Characters —

Capulet family and friends:

JULIET CAPULET: A 13-year-old girl

LORD CAPULET: Juliet's father and the enemy of Lord Montague

LADY CAPULET: Juliet's mother

NURSE: Juliet's nanny

SAMPSON and **GREGORY:** Lord Capulet's servants

TYBALT: Juliet's cousin

PARIS: A young man who wants to marry Juliet; Prince Escalus's cousin

PRINCE ESCALUS: Prince and ruler of Verona

— The Prologue —

*(The **Chorus** enters.)*

CHORUS: This play is about two families in Verona, Italy. They have been fighting for years. Two teens fall in love. One is a Capulet. The other is a Montague. They take their own lives. The fighting stops. Read on. You will learn the details.

ACT 1

— Scene 1 —

*(A Verona street. **Sampson** and **Gregory** enter. They have swords. They are looking for trouble.)*

SAMPSON: I won't be put down by Montagues. Believe me!

GREGORY: Calm down. This isn't our

fight. The fight is between our bosses.

SAMPSON: It's all the same to me. I would fight any of them.

GREGORY: Here's your chance. Draw your sword!

SAMPSON *(drawing his sword)***:** Pick a fight with them. I'll back you up.

GREGORY: How? By running away?

SAMPSON: Don't worry!

GREGORY: I'm more afraid of what you will do. I'm not afraid of the Montagues.

SAMPSON: We'll let them start the fight. Then we'll have a right to fight back. The law will be on our side.

GREGORY: I'll frown as they pass by. They can take it however they want.

SAMPSON: I'll make a face at them. They'll

have to fight. Or they'll be shamed.

*(**Abraham** and **Balthazar** enter.)*

ABRAHAM: Did you make a face at us?

SAMPSON *(aside to Gregory)*: What will happen if I say yes? Will we be arrested?

GREGORY: Yes.

SAMPSON: Then, no. I didn't make a face at you.

GREGORY: Do you want to fight?

ABRAHAM: Fight? No, sir!

SAMPSON: Well, if you do, I'm ready. My boss is as good as yours.

ABRAHAM: As good? Maybe. But no better.

GREGORY: Say "better"—here comes Benvolio. He'll back us up.

SAMPSON: Yes, say "better"!

ABRAHAM: You lie!

SAMPSON: Draw your swords. Gregory, are you ready?

*(They fight. **Benvolio** enters.)*

BENVOLIO: Stop, fools! Put away your swords. You don't know what you're doing.

*(He beats down their swords. **Tybalt** enters.)*

TYBALT: Are you fighting with the servants?

BENVOLIO: No, I'm trying to stop the fight. Put your sword away. Or use it to help me stop it.

TYBALT: Are you talking about peace with your sword drawn? I hate the Montagues. I hate you! Come on, coward!

*(They fight. **Others** join in. **Lord** and **Lady** **Capulet** enter.)*

CAPULET: What's going on? Give me a sword too.

LADY CAPULET: You need a crutch, not a sword.

CAPULET: Give me my sword! Montague is coming. He's waving his sword to make me mad.

11

*(**Lord** and **Lady Montague** enter.)*

MONTAGUE: I hate you, Capulet!

(to his wife, who is holding him back):
Let me at him!

LADY MONTAGUE: Stop! I will not let
you do this.

*(**Prince Escalus** and his **men** arrive.)*

PRINCE: Rebels, listen! Drop your swords
and listen to me. This is the third time
you have fought in our streets. If you do
this again, you will pay with your lives.
Clear the streets!

Capulet, come with me. Montague, I will
meet with you this afternoon. You will die
if I catch you fighting one more time.

*(**Everyone** leaves except the Montagues and
Benvolio.)*

MONTAGUE: Who started this fight, nephew?

BENVOLIO: I saw Capulet's servants fighting with yours. I tried to stop them. Tybalt came in and drew his sword. The crowd joined in. Then the Prince came and stopped it.

LADY MONTAGUE: Where is Romeo? I'm glad he wasn't in this fight.

BENVOLIO: I saw him earlier. He was in the woods. I walked toward him. When he saw me, he ran and hid. I didn't follow him.

MONTAGUE: He goes there a lot to cry. When it's light, he hides in his room. I wish we knew what was wrong. We would gladly help him.

BENVOLIO: Here he comes. I'll see if I can find out anything.

MONTAGUE: I hope you can.

*(**Lord** and **Lady Montague** leave. **Romeo** enters.)*

BENVOLIO: Good morning, cousin.

ROMEO: Is it still morning? Sad hours drag on so! Was that my father who just left?

BENVOLIO: It was. Tell me what makes you so sad.

ROMEO: Love. I want love. The woman I love will not love me back. What a waste. Her beauty will die with her.

BENVOLIO: She has sworn she will not get married?

ROMEO: She has. It seems such a waste. It makes me feel like dying.

BENVOLIO: Listen, cousin. Forget her!

ROMEO: Teach me how to do that!

BENVOLIO: You must look at other beautiful ladies.

ROMEO: It won't work. I would only think of her. She is more beautiful than anyone else. You can't teach me to forget her!

BENVOLIO: I will. Or I'll die trying!

*(**Romeo** and **Benvolio** leave.)*

— Scene 2 —

*(**Lord Capulet**, **Paris**, and a **servant** enter the street.)*

CAPULET: Montague must obey the Prince too. It shouldn't be hard to keep the peace.

PARIS: You are both men of honor. It's sad this fighting goes on. But I have come to ask you a question. May I marry your daughter, Juliet?

CAPULET: I say what I have said before. She is too young to marry. She isn't 14 yet. Wait two more years. Then I will allow her to marry.

PARIS: Many girls younger than Juliet have become happy mothers.

CAPULET: Those girls grow up too fast. My other children are dead. Juliet is the only child I have left. You may charm her, Paris. Be kind to her. It is up to her. If she agrees, I will let you marry her.

Tonight, I'm having a dinner party. I've invited many guests. You are welcome to come too. You will see many beautiful women there. You may fall in love with someone else.

*(to the servant, giving him a piece of paper)***:** Go ask these people to the party.

*(**Paris** and **Capulet** leave.)*

SERVANT *(aside)***:** *Go ask these people!* He's forgotten I can't read. I need to find someone to help me.

*(**Romeo** and **Benvolio** enter.)*

BENVOLIO: I'll tell you what you need to do. Fall in love with someone else. You'll soon forget her.

ROMEO: Nothing can help me, Benvolio.

*(to the servant)***:** Hello.

SERVANT: Hello, sir. Can you read?

ROMEO: Yes, I can read my own sad future.

SERVANT: You can read that without a book. But can you read words?

ROMEO: Yes.

SERVANT *(hands Romeo the list)***:** Please read this.

ROMEO *(reading list)***:** That's quite a group.

(He returns the list.) Where's the party?

SERVANT: At Lord Capulet's house. If you're not a Montague, you can come. Good-bye now.

*(**Servant** leaves.)*

BENVOLIO: Rosaline will be there. Go to the party. You'll see other beautiful women. Then you'll think your swan is a crow.

ROMEO: There is no one more beautiful!

BENVOLIO: How do you know? You have never compared her to another. Tonight, look at some of the other girls. Rosaline is not the only girl in Verona. I'll show you.

ROMEO: I'll go. I will enjoy seeing my beautiful Rosaline.

*(**Romeo** and **Benvolio** leave.)*

— Scene 3 —

(A room in Capulet's house. **Lady Capulet** *and* **Nurse** *enter.)*

LADY CAPULET: Nurse, where's my daughter? Call her.

NURSE: Juliet!

*(**Juliet** enters.)*

JULIET: Who wants to see me?

NURSE: Your mother.

JULIET: Hello, Mother. What is your wish?

LADY CAPULET: Nurse, leave us now. No, wait! I want you to hear this too. You know my daughter's age.

NURSE: Of course. I can tell her age to the hour.

LADY CAPULET: She's not 14.

NURSE: She will be 14 in about two weeks. It's hard to believe. She was the most beautiful baby I have ever taken care of. I hope I live long enough to see her get married.

LADY CAPULET: That is what I want to talk about.

*(to Juliet)***:** How do you feel about getting married?

JULIET: I haven't thought much about it.

LADY CAPULET: Well, think about it. Many girls your age are mothers. I was a mother when I was your age. Did you know that Paris would like to marry you?

NURSE: What luck, Juliet! He's a fine man!

LADY CAPULET: There is no finer man in Verona.

NURSE: He's a great man!

LADY CAPULET: What do you say? Can you love him? He'll be at the party tonight. Look at him. If you marry him, you will have all that he has. You will better yourself. Do you think you could love Paris?

JULIET: I will take a look at him. But only because you ask. If I like him, I will think about marrying him.

*(A **servant** enters.)*

SERVANT: The guests are here.

LADY CAPULET: We will follow you.

*(**Servant** leaves.)*

Juliet, Paris is waiting for you.

NURSE: Go, my girl!

*(**All** leave.)*

— Scene 4 —

*(**Romeo**, **Mercutio**, and **Benvolio** are in the street. They are wearing party masks.)*

ROMEO: Should we just go in quietly?

BENVOLIO: We don't have to say a thing. We'll have one dance. Then we'll leave.

ROMEO: I don't feel like dancing. I am in a dark mood. I will carry the torch.

MERCUTIO: You must dance!

ROMEO: I'm too sad to dance.

MERCUTIO: You're in love. You should be happy. You should fly!

ROMEO: Love is a heavy load. I can't move.

MERCUTIO: That's a strange way to describe love. It's a tender thing.

ROMEO: Is love a tender thing? To me, it's hard. It cuts like a thorn.

MERCUTIO: If love is hard on you, be hard on love. Beat it down. We're almost there.

BENVOLIO: Here we are. Knock and enter. As soon as we're in, start dancing.

ROMEO: I'll just watch.

MERCUTIO: We'll get you out of this bad mood. Come on.

ROMEO: I don't think it's a good idea to go to this party.

MERCUTIO: Why?

ROMEO: I had a dream last night.

MERCUTIO: Ah, Queen Mab came to visit you. She's the fairy of dreams. She makes lovers dream of love. And lawyers dream of money. And ladies dream of kisses.

ROMEO: Enough. Stop. You're full of it.

MERCUTIO: True. I'm talking about dreams. They're nothing.

ROMEO: Something bad is going to happen. I feel like I might die. Time will tell. Let's go.

*(**All** leave.)*

— Scene 5 —

*(A hall in Capulet's house. Musicians are waiting. **Servants** enter.)*

FIRST SERVANT: Where is Potpan? He should be helping us clean up.

SECOND SERVANT: You can't count on Potpan.

FIRST SERVANT: Take the chairs away. Take the table.

*(**Second servant** leaves. **Lord** and **Lady Capulet** enter. **Juliet**, **Tybalt**, **Nurse**, **guests**, and **musicians** enter.)*

CAPULET: Welcome, guests! Everyone must dance. I remember wearing a mask and dancing. Those days are gone! Come, musicians, play!

(Music plays. Everyone dances.)

More light! Move those tables! Put out the fire. The room's too hot. Hello, cousin Capulet. How long has it been since we have danced?

COUSIN CAPULET: Thirty years!

CAPULET: I don't believe it! I think it has only been 25.

COUSIN CAPULET: It's longer.

CAPULET: It can't be true.

ROMEO *(to a servant)*: Who's that lady?

SERVANT: I don't know, sir.

ROMEO: She's like a white dove among crows. She shines like the stars. I've never seen anyone so beautiful.

TYBALT: I know that voice! He's a Montague! Why is he here? I'll kill him.

CAPULET: Tybalt! Why are you so angry?

TYBALT: Uncle, that man is a Montague. He's our enemy. He has come to spoil the party.

CAPULET: Is it Romeo?

TYBALT: Yes, it is. He's bad.

CAPULET: Calm down. Let him stay. He looks like a good man. I will not be rude to him. It's no way to behave at a party.

TYBALT: But he's our enemy. I don't want him to stay.

CAPULET: You are the one spoiling the party. Either go away or be quiet.

TYBALT: Fine, I'll leave. But I won't forget.

(Tybalt leaves.)

ROMEO *(to Juliet)***:** If my hand is too rough, I'll soothe yours with a kiss.

JULIET: Your hand is fine. Don't people

pray by touching their hands together?

ROMEO: Yes, and we also pray with our lips. Let's touch our lips together.

(They kiss.)

NURSE: Juliet, your mother would like to see you.

(Juliet moves away.)

ROMEO: Who is her mother?

NURSE: Lady Capulet. Whoever marries Juliet will be rich.

ROMEO *(to Benvolio)***:** She is a Capulet. Oh no! My life is in my foe's hands.

BENVOLIO: Let's go. The party is over.

ROMEO: Yes, that's sad.

CAPULET: Don't go. Have more food. Must you leave? Thanks for coming.

*(**All** leave but Juliet and Nurse.)*

JULIET: Nurse, please come here. Who is that young man?

NURSE: I don't know.

JULIET: Go. Find out his name. If he's married, I will die!

*(**Nurse** leaves, then returns.)*

NURSE: His name is Romeo. He's a Montague. He is the only son of your family's enemy.

JULIET: My only love comes from my only hate. Why is this happening? Now it's too late! I love my family's enemy.

NURSE: Let's go to bed. Everyone is gone.

*(**Juliet** and **Nurse** leave.)*

Act 2

— Scene 1 —

(Outside the wall of Capulet's garden. **Romeo** *enters.)*

ROMEO: I can't leave. My heart is here!

*(**Romeo** climbs the wall.)*

*(**Benvolio** and **Mercutio** enter.)*

BENVOLIO: Romeo, where are you?

MERCUTIO: I think he's gone home.

BENVOLIO: I think he ran this way. He jumped over the wall. Call him, Mercutio.

MERCUTIO: Romeo? Madman! Lover! Call to us.

(Mercutio listens. Romeo doesn't answer.)

I'll say the magic word: Rosaline. Oh, Romeo! By Rosaline's bright eyes, I call you to come to us!

BENVOLIO *(laughing)***:** If he hears you, he'll be angry.

MERCUTIO: This cannot anger him. I used his lover's name to get his attention.

BENVOLIO: He's hiding in the trees. His love is blind. He sees better in the dark.

MERCUTIO: Come on, let's leave him alone. Good night, Romeo.

BENVOLIO: Let's go, then. It's foolish to look for him. He doesn't want to be found.

*(**Benvolio** and **Mercutio** leave.)*

— Scene 2 —

*(Capulet's garden. **Romeo** enters.)*

ROMEO: Mercutio laughs at my problems. He doesn't know how it feels. He's never been in love.

*(**Juliet** comes to the window.)*

Wait. What's that light in the window? It is the east. And Juliet is the sun. Rise, beautiful sun. Kill the jealous moon. The moon is pale and sad. Because Juliet is more beautiful.

There's Juliet. It's her. If only she knew how I feel. She speaks. But she says nothing. Her eyes speak. But not to me.

Two bright stars had to go away. They ask Juliet's eyes to twinkle in their place. Her bright eyes would make the sky so light. Birds would sing, thinking it wasn't night.

Look at her cheek. It's resting on her hand. Oh, I wish I were a glove. Then I could touch her cheek.

JULIET: Oh my!

ROMEO: She speaks! Speak again. You are like an angel to me.

JULIET: Oh, Romeo, why are you a Montague? Change your name. Or just say you love me. I will no longer be a Capulet.

ROMEO *(aside)***:** Should I talk now?

JULIET: Only your name is my enemy. You would be the same man if you weren't a Montague. What does a name mean, anyway? A rose would still smell sweet no matter what we call it. Romeo, trade your name in and take all of me.

ROMEO: Love me. I'll never be called Romeo again.

JULIET: Who's there? Why are you hiding in the dark?

ROMEO: I don't want to tell you my name. I hate my name.

JULIET: Aren't you Romeo Montague?

ROMEO: Not if it makes you unhappy.

JULIET: How did you get in here? You are in danger.

ROMEO: My love for you gave me wings. I flew over the wall. I'm not afraid.

JULIET: If they see you, they'll kill you.

ROMEO: Just look sweetly at me. I'll be ready for them.

JULIET: I don't want them to see you here.

ROMEO: They won't see me. It's too dark. I don't want to live without your love. I would rather be killed.

JULIET: Who told you how to find me?

ROMEO: Love told me. I would go anywhere to find you.

JULIET: Did you hear what I said about you? I'm blushing. Do you love me? I know you'll say yes. I will believe you. I can't pretend to be shy. I love you.

ROMEO: I swear by the moon—

JULIET: Don't swear by the moon. It changes from one night to the next.

ROMEO: What should I swear by?

JULIET: Swear by your kind self. I'll believe you.

ROMEO: I swear—

JULIET: No, don't. You give me joy. But I am not happy about our love. It's moving too fast! Good night! Sleep well.

ROMEO: Will you leave me sad?

JULIET: What happiness can you have tonight?

ROMEO: I want you to promise your love to me.

JULIET: I loved you as soon as I saw you. But I wish I could take it back.

ROMEO: Why?

JULIET: So that I could give it to you over and over again. My love is as deep as the sea. The more I give you, the more I have. It is endless.

*(Offstage, **Nurse** calls.)*

JULIET: Stay a minute. I'll be right back.

*(**Juliet** leaves.)*

ROMEO: What a blessed night. I fear that it is only a dream. It's too sweet to be real.

*(**Juliet** comes back.)*

JULIET: I can only stay a minute. If you want to marry me, send word tomorrow. Tell me where to meet you. I'll follow you anywhere.

NURSE *(offstage)***:** Juliet!

JULIET: I've got to go. If you don't want

to marry me, leave me alone. But I'll be so sad. Good night!

(*Juliet* leaves.)

ROMEO: She's gone. This is terrible.

(*Juliet* comes back.)

JULIET: Romeo! What time shall I send for you tomorrow?

ROMEO: At nine.

JULIET: I'll do it. It's such a long time from now. Parting is so sad. Good night, my love.

(*Juliet* leaves.)

ROMEO: Sleep well, my love. I will go see Friar Lawrence. I have to tell him the good news.

(*Romeo* leaves.)

— Scene 3 —

*(**Friar Lawrence** enters his room. He is holding a basket.)*

FRIAR LAWRENCE: Morning is here. It's getting lighter. I must fill these baskets with plants. Or it will get too hot. The earth is nature's mother. But also nature's grave.

Plants have great power. There's some good in everything. But good can be abused. Good becomes bad if misused. This plant can both help and harm. Smelling it will make you well. Tasting it will kill you. There's good and evil in everything.

*(**Romeo** enters.)*

ROMEO: Good morning, Father!

FRIAR LAWRENCE: Bless you! Why are you up so early? Is something wrong?

ROMEO: Yes. I can't sleep.

FRIAR LAWRENCE: Were you with Rosaline?

ROMEO: No, I've forgotten about her.

FRIAR LAWRENCE: Good, my son. But where have you been?

ROMEO: I went to a party at Capulet's house. One of them hurt me. And I hurt her. You can help make us feel better.

FRIAR LAWRENCE: You are speaking in riddles. I don't understand.

ROMEO: I love Capulet's daughter. She loves me too. We want to be married! Please marry us today.

FRIAR LAWRENCE: My goodness! Have you forgotten Rosaline so quickly? I can't believe it. What's changed?

ROMEO: You often scolded me for loving Rosaline. You told me to forget her.

FRIAR LAWRENCE: But I didn't tell you to love another.

ROMEO: Juliet loves me. Rosaline did not.

FRIAR LAWRENCE: All right. I will help you. Maybe this wedding will stop all the fighting.

ROMEO: Let's go! I want this done quickly.

FRIAR LAWRENCE: Go slowly. If you run, you might fall.

*(**Romeo** and **Friar Lawrence** leave.)*

— Scene 4 —

*(A street. **Benvolio** and **Mercutio** enter.)*

MERCUTIO: Where is Romeo? Did he come home last night?

BENVOLIO: No.

MERCUTIO: He must still be sad about Rosaline.

BENVOLIO: Tybalt, a Capulet cousin, sent a letter to Romeo's house.

MERCUTIO: I'll bet he's asking Romeo to fight him.

BENVOLIO: Romeo will fight Tybalt.

MERCUTIO: He's been hit by Cupid's arrow. Is he strong enough to fight? He won't win.

BENVOLIO: Why, what's Tybalt deal?

MERCUTIO: He's an expert with a sword. He can slice a button off a shirt.

(Romeo enters.)

BENVOLIO: Here comes Romeo!

MERCUTIO: Good morning, Romeo. We lost you last night.

ROMEO: Good morning to you both. I'm sorry for last night. I had some business to take care of. Everything is good now.

MERCUTIO: Who's coming?

(Nurse enters.)

NURSE: Good morning, gentlemen. Where can I find Romeo?

ROMEO: I am Romeo.

NURSE: I need to talk with you.

ROMEO *(to Benvolio and Mercutio)*: Friends, go to my father's house. I will meet you later.

*(**Mercutio** and **Benvolio** leave.)*

NURSE: Juliet asked me to find you. First, though, let me tell you something. She is a young and good woman. If you are lying about your love, you will have to deal with me!

ROMEO: Nurse, please tell Juliet hello. I promise—

NURSE: Bless your heart! I can tell you are true. She'll be so happy.

ROMEO: Tell her to meet me this afternoon at the church. Friar Lawrence will marry us today.

NURSE: She will be there, sir.

ROMEO: One more thing. My servant will meet you. He will bring a ladder. Hide it near Juliet's window. I will climb up to her room tonight. Can you keep our secret?

NURSE: I can. Can you trust your servant?

ROMEO: I trust him.

NURSE: Juliet is very sweet. Count Paris would like to marry her. But she doesn't love him. She loves you.

ROMEO: Give her my love.

NURSE: Yes, I will.

*(**Romeo** and **Nurse** leave.)*

— Scene 5 —

*(Capulet's garden. **Juliet** enters.)*

JULIET: Where is she? She said she'd be back by now. What's wrong? Maybe she couldn't find Romeo. She's so slow. Oh! Here she comes.

*(**Nurse** enters.)*

Sweet nurse, give me the news. Have you met with him?

NURSE: Wait a minute. Let me rest.

JULIET: Please, I can't wait any longer! Is it good news or bad?

NURSE: Your love says ... He's a gentleman. Handsome too. Where is your mother?

JULIET: Where is my mother? She's inside. What does Romeo want with my mother?

NURSE: Now you're angry. Is this how you repay me? From now on, tend to your own business. Don't ask me to help you.

JULIET: Please tell me what he said.

NURSE: Are you allowed to go to church today?

JULIET: Yes.

NURSE: Then go see Friar Lawrence. Romeo will meet you there. The friar will marry the two of you. I must go get a ladder. Romeo will use it to climb to your room when it is dark.

JULIET: What good news! Thank you.

*(**Nurse** and **Juliet** leave.)*

— Scene 6 —

*(**Friar Lawrence** and **Romeo** enter the friar's room.)*

FRIAR LAWRENCE: May heaven smile on this holy act. May it not cause any sadness.

ROMEO: But if something bad happens, it won't take away my joy. I am happy just looking at her. If I die, I will die a happy man. I am happy that I can call her mine.

FRIAR LAWRENCE: A rapid love will die quickly. Love slowly. It will last longer.

*(**Juliet** enters. Romeo kisses her.)*

FRIAR LAWRENCE: Here is the lady. I think their love will last.

ROMEO: Juliet, are you as happy as I am? Tell me how you feel.

JULIET: Yes! My love has grown so much. I feel rich!

FRIAR LAWRENCE: Come with me. We will do this quickly.

*(**Romeo**, **Juliet**, and **Friar Lawrence** leave.)*

Act 3

— Scene 1 —

*(**Mercutio** and **Benvolio** enter the street.)*

BENVOLIO: Mercutio, let's go home. The Capulets are around. If we meet, there will be a fight.

MERCUTIO: You are always looking for a fight.

BENVOLIO: Am I?

MERCUTIO: Yes, it's easy to make you angry. You will fight about anything.

BENVOLIO: If I fought as much as you, I would already be dead.

MERCUTIO: Ha-ha! You said it. I didn't!

BENVOLIO: Here come the Capulets.

MERCUTIO: I don't care.

*(**Tybalt** and **others** enter the street.)*

TYBALT *(to his friends)*: Stay close. I'm going to talk to them.

(to Benvolio and Mercutio): Can I speak with you?

MERCUTIO: Just talk? We should fight!

TYBALT: I'm ready if you are. You are in Romeo's band—

MERCUTIO: Band? You make us sound as if we play music.

(waving his sword): Here, dance to the tune of my sword.

BENVOLIO: Everyone is looking. Go somewhere private if you're going to fight.

MERCUTIO: Let them look! I don't care.

TYBALT: Well, peace be with you, sir.

*(**Romeo** enters.)*

Here comes the man I've been looking for. Romeo, you are a creep!

ROMEO: I will pretend you didn't say that. You don't really know me. Good-bye.

TYBALT: I can't forget all the hurt you have caused me. Turn and draw your sword.

ROMEO: I have never hurt you. I love the name Capulet. Calm down.

MERCUTIO: What are you saying, Romeo?

(He draws his sword.)

Tybalt, you rat-catcher, fight me.

TYBALT: What do you want with me?

MERCUTIO: Your life!

TYBALT *(draws his sword)*: I am ready for you!

ROMEO: Mercutio, put your sword away. Remember what the Prince said. If we are caught fighting, we will die. Stop, Tybalt. Please, Mercutio!

(Mercutio and Tybalt fight. Romeo steps between them. Tybalt wounds Mercutio. **Tybalt** *runs away.)*

MERCUTIO: I'm hurt. I'm dying! A curse on both your families.

BENVOLIO: Are you hurt?

MERCUTIO: Yes! Where's my servant? Go get a doctor.

*(**Servant** leaves.)*

ROMEO: Be brave, Mercutio.

MERCUTIO: It's not so bad. But I will

be dead tomorrow. Why did you come between us? He struck me by going under your arm.

ROMEO: I thought I was doing the best thing.

MERCUTIO: Help me into a house, Benvolio. A curse on both your families!

(***Mercutio*** *and* ***Benvolio*** *leave.*)

55

ROMEO: My friend's been hurt because Tybalt insulted me. Tybalt is now my relative. Juliet, your love makes me weak.

(Benvolio returns.)

BENVOLIO: Romeo, Mercutio is dead!

ROMEO: This is a black day. It's just the beginning. More sad days will follow.

BENVOLIO: Tybalt is back again!

ROMEO: Tybalt is alive. Mercutio is dead!

(Tybalt enters.)

You're the evil one. One of us must die.

(Romeo and Tybalt fight. Tybalt falls dead.)

BENVOLIO: Romeo, run away! People are coming. The Prince will have you put to death. Run!

ROMEO: Oh, I have bad luck.

BENVOLIO: Why are you still here? Run!

(**Romeo** runs. The **Prince** arrives followed by **Montagues**, **Capulets**, and **others**.)

PRINCE: Who started this fight?

BENVOLIO: I can tell you. Tybalt killed Mercutio. Then Romeo killed Tybalt.

LADY CAPULET: Oh, my nephew! A Capulet has been killed. A Montague must die.

PRINCE: Benvolio, what happened?

BENVOLIO: Tybalt started the fight. Romeo tried to stop it. But Tybalt wouldn't listen. Mercutio tried to defend Romeo. Tybalt killed him. Romeo was angry. He killed Tybalt. Then he ran.

LADY CAPULET: He's lying to save Romeo. Romeo killed Tybalt. Romeo must die.

PRINCE: But Tybalt killed Mercutio. Who should pay for that?

MONTAGUE: Well, not Romeo. He was Mercutio's friend. Tybalt got what he deserved. Romeo did what the law would have done. He killed Tybalt.

PRINCE: I'll send Romeo away. He will never be allowed to return to our city. Mercutio was my relative too. I'll charge a huge fine. Let Romeo go. If we find him here, we will kill him. Killers must be punished. Or more murders will happen.

(All leave.)

— Scene 2 —

*(A room in the Capulet house. **Juliet** enters.)*

JULIET: I wish night would come quickly. Then Romeo will be in my arms. Come, night. Come, Romeo. I can't wait! Oh, here comes my nurse. I hope she has some good news.

*(**Nurse** enters with a rope ladder.)*

NURSE: Here is the rope ladder Romeo wanted.

(She throws down the ladder.)

JULIET: Oh my! What's the news? You look worried.

NURSE: He's dead. He's dead. He's dead! We are finished! He's gone.

JULIET: Why are you telling me this?

You are torturing me. Has Romeo killed himself?

NURSE: I saw his dead body with my own eyes. He was covered in blood. I fainted.

JULIET: My heart is broken. I must die with him.

NURSE: Tybalt was the best friend I ever had. I can't believe he's dead.

JULIET: Are Romeo and Tybalt both dead?

NURSE: Tybalt is dead. Romeo must leave Verona. He can never return.

JULIET: Did Romeo kill Tybalt?

NURSE: He did.

JULIET: He is a snake! He's evil! His looks are a good mask. I never would guess he could kill someone.

NURSE: All men are liars! Shame on Romeo!

JULIET: Don't say that! He is an honest man. I should never have said those terrible things.

NURSE: How can you forgive your cousin's killer?

JULIET: He is my husband. I must be true to him. Why did he kill Tybalt? Tybalt must have tried to kill him. I'm glad Romeo is alive. Then why am I crying? I may never see him again. Where are my mother and father?

NURSE: They are crying over Tybalt's body. Do you want to see them? I will take you there.

JULIET: I am crying over Romeo. Death will be my husband now.

NURSE: Go to your room. I'll find Romeo to calm you. I know where he is. He is with Friar Lawrence.

JULIET: Oh, find him! Give him this ring. Tell him to come and say good-bye.

*(**Both** leave.)*

— Scene 3 —

*(**Friar Lawrence** enters his room.)*

FRIAR LAWRENCE: Romeo, come out. You are scared. And you are married to trouble.

ROMEO: What is my punishment for killing Tybalt?

FRIAR LAWRENCE: Your luck is all bad. The Prince said you must leave Verona and never return.

ROMEO: That is worse than death to me.

FRIAR LAWRENCE: The Prince has spared your life. You should thank him.

ROMEO: Heaven is here in Verona. Where Juliet lives. Do you have some poison? A sharp knife? I want to die.

FRIAR LAWRENCE: You foolish man. Listen to me. I will comfort you.

ROMEO: Nothing you can say will comfort me.

FRIAR LAWRENCE: Listen to me!

ROMEO: You can't feel what I feel. If you killed her cousin? Then you could talk about it. Then you could tear out your hair. Then you could fall on the ground like me. Then you can measure your grave.

(Knocking from offstage.)

FRIAR LAWRENCE: Hide, Romeo! Someone is knocking.

ROMEO: No!

(More knocking.)

FRIAR LAWRENCE: Who's there?

Romeo, get up! Stand up. Hide. Who's knocking? What do you want?

NURSE *(from offstage)*: Let me in. I have news from Lady Juliet.

FRIAR LAWRENCE *(opening the door)*: Welcome, then.

*(**Nurse** enters.)*

NURSE: Father, please tell me, where is Romeo?

FRIAR LAWRENCE: Over there on the floor. He is very sad.

NURSE: He is acting just like Juliet. Fussing and crying! Stand up! Be a man, for Juliet's sake.

ROMEO *(rising from the floor)*: Nurse! How is Juliet? Does she hate me for killing Tybalt? Where is she? What does she say about our love?

NURSE: She says nothing. She just weeps. She calls for Tybalt. She calls for Romeo. Then she falls on her bed.

ROMEO: My name has killed her. Just as I have killed her cousin. Father, tell me where is my name inside my body? I want to cut it out!

FRIAR LAWRENCE: Calm down! Are you a man? You're acting like a young girl. You're like a wild beast! Will you kill yourself? Then you will kill your wife too. The two of you are one now. Juliet is alive. You are blessed. If you had not killed Tybalt, he would have killed you. You are alive! Be happy! Go to Juliet. Comfort her.

Then go to Mantua. Hide there. When the time is right, we will announce your marriage. We will beg the Prince to pardon you. Everyone will be happy. Nurse, go tell Juliet that Romeo is coming.

NURSE: I'll tell her.

*(**Nurse** leaves.)*

ROMEO: I feel better. It's a good plan.

FRIAR LAWRENCE: Remember you must leave before dawn. Wait in Mantua. I'll send your servant to you with news. Good-bye, Romeo.

ROMEO: Thank you, Father. Good-bye.

*(**Friar Lawrence** and **Romeo** leave.)*

— Scene 4 —

*(The **Capulets** enter a room in their house with **Paris**.)*

CAPULET: We haven't had time to talk to Juliet about you, Paris. She doesn't know you wish to marry her. She won't come down tonight. It's very late.

PARIS: Please don't bother her now. Just tell her I asked about her.

LADY CAPULET: I will tell her tomorrow. She is too sad tonight.

CAPULET: I think you should marry her soon. My daughter will do what I tell her. Wife, go tell Juliet the news. What day is this?

PARIS: Monday.

CAPULET: The wedding will be Thursday.

(to his wife): Tell her she will marry Paris on Thursday.

(to Paris): We'll have a small wedding. Will you be ready?

PARIS: I wish Thursday were tomorrow.

CAPULET: Thursday it will be.

(to his wife): Go to Juliet. Prepare her.

(to Paris): Good night, my lord. It is so late.

*(They **all** leave.)*

— Scene 5 —

*(**Romeo** and **Juliet** stand on the balcony.)*

JULIET: Will you leave? It's not morning yet.

ROMEO: See the light in the east. I must leave and live. If I stay, I will die.

JULIET: That is not daylight. I know it. So stay a while. You don't have to go yet.

ROMEO: You know I want to stay. I will welcome death. If that is what you want. Talk to me, Juliet. It is not yet day.

JULIET: It is! Go, then. It is getting lighter.

ROMEO: The lighter it gets, the sadder I feel.

*(**Nurse** enters.)*

NURSE: Your mother is coming! It's morning. Be careful.

*(**Nurse** leaves.)*

JULIET: Window, let day in. Let life out.

ROMEO: Give me one kiss. Then I'll leave.

(They kiss. Romeo climbs down to the garden.)

JULIET: Have you left? I must hear from you every day.

ROMEO: I will send word soon. Good-bye, my love.

JULIET: Do you think we'll ever meet again?

ROMEO: Yes, I know we will. Then these troubles will give us stories to tell.

JULIET: I have a bad feeling. I can see you in your grave. Are my eyes playing tricks on me? You look pale.

ROMEO: My love, you look pale too. It must be sadness. Good-bye!

(Romeo leaves.)

JULIET: Oh, luck. Send him back soon.

(Lady Capulet enters.)

LADY CAPULET: Juliet, are you up?

JULIET: Yes, but I am not well.

LADY CAPULET: Are you still crying over Tybalt? Your tears won't bring him back. Stop crying. I have good news for you!

JULIET: Joy is welcome at this sad time. What is it?

LADY CAPULET: Your father loves you very much. He has planned your marriage to Paris. On Thursday, you will be his bride!

JULIET: I will not! I don't even know

him. Tell my father that I will not marry yet. When I'm ready, I'll marry Romeo. Never Paris! This is not good news!

LADY CAPULET: Here comes your father. You can tell him yourself.

*(**Capulet** and **Nurse** enter.)*

CAPULET: Why are you still crying, my dear? Wife, have you told her the good news?

LADY CAPULET: I have. She says no.

CAPULET: What do you mean, she says no? Doesn't she thank us? Doesn't she feel lucky? I have found a fine man for her.

JULIET: I will never marry Paris.

LADY CAPULET: Are you crazy?

JULIET: Please listen to me. I beg you.

CAPULET: I won't listen! You will be married to Paris on Thursday. If not, you will never see me again. Wife, this daughter is a curse!

NURSE: You are too angry.

CAPULET: I am angry! I have worked hard to find her a good man. And she says no. Juliet, if you don't marry Paris, you will not live here. You can die in the streets. Think about it.

(Capulet leaves.)

JULIET: Is there no pity for me? Mother, please help me. Please delay this wedding. If you don't, I will die.

LADY CAPULET: Quiet! I am done with you.

(Lady Capulet leaves.)

JULIET: Nurse, what can I do? I am already

married to Romeo. Tell me what to do.

NURSE: You might never see Romeo again. He is as good as dead. Use your head. Marry Paris. He's a better match for you.

JULIET: Do you think so?

NURSE: Yes, I do.

JULIET: You have helped me. Go and tell my parents I am sorry. Tell them that I have gone to confession. I want to be forgiven.

NURSE: I will. You are very wise to do this.

*(**Nurse** leaves.)*

JULIET *(aside)***:** Crazy old lady. She is no help. First she praises Romeo. Then she puts him down. I will never tell her my secrets again. I'll ask the friar what I should do.

*(**Juliet** leaves.)*

Act 4

— Scene 1 —

*(**Friar Lawrence** and **Paris** enter the friar's room.)*

FRIAR LAWRENCE: The wedding will be on Thursday? Why so soon?

PARIS: Lord Capulet wants it that way.

FRIAR LAWRENCE: What does Juliet say? I don't like this. It's not right.

PARIS: She is still crying over Tybalt. We have not had a chance to get to know each other. Her father thinks it will be good for her to get married. He wants her to be happy.

*(**Juliet** enters.)*

PARIS: Hello, my wife.

JULIET: I'm not your wife yet.

PARIS: But you will be on Thursday.

JULIET: What must be will be.

FRIAR LAWRENCE: That's true.

PARIS: Have you come to confession?

JULIET: I can't tell you what I will tell him.

PARIS: Tell him that you love me.

JULIET: I will tell you that I love him.

PARIS: And I'm sure you will say you love me.

JULIET: It will mean more if I say it behind your back. Father, are you free now?

FRIAR LAWRENCE: Yes, my dear. Paris, Juliet and I must talk alone.

PARIS: Yes, of course. Juliet, I will come for you on Thursday.

*(**Paris** kisses her and leaves.)*

JULIET: Father, shut the door. Weep with me. I have no hope!

FRIAR LAWRENCE: I hear you must marry Paris on Thursday.

JULIET: Don't tell me what you have heard. If you can't help me, I will kill myself with this knife.

(She takes out a knife. She shows it to him.)

You married us. My heart is joined with Romeo's. Please tell me what to do. I'll kill myself before I will marry Paris!

FRIAR LAWRENCE: I see some hope. If you are brave enough, I'll give you an answer.

JULIET: I would leap from a tower to keep from marrying Paris! I'll do anything!

FRIAR LAWRENCE: Go tell your parents you will marry Paris. Tomorrow night, drink this potion. It will make you look dead. Paris will find you. He will take you to the tomb.

While you sleep, I will write to Romeo. He will come when you wake up. He'll take you to Mantua. This will solve your problem. Unless you are afraid.

JULIET: Give it to me! I have no fear!

FRIAR LAWRENCE: Go home. Be strong. I'll write to your husband.

JULIET: Thank you, Father!

(They leave.)

— Scene 2 —

(Lord and Lady Capulet, Nurse, and servants enter a hall in the Capulet's house.)

CAPULET: Invite all the people on this list.

(He hands a paper to first servant, who leaves.)

Hire me some cooks.

SECOND SERVANT: Yes, sir. I will choose the best.

CAPULET: How will you know they are good?

SECOND SERVANT: Simple. A bad cook won't lick his own fingers.

CAPULET: Go. Be gone.

(Second servant leaves.)

We are not ready for this wedding. Has Juliet gone to see Friar Lawrence?

NURSE: Yes, sir.

CAPULET: Maybe he can help her. She's so stubborn.

*(**Juliet** comes in.)*

CAPULET: My stubborn child! Where have you been?

JULIET: I went to see Friar Lawrence. I told him I was sorry for not obeying your wishes. He told me to ask you to forgive me. I'm sorry, Father. I will obey you.

CAPULET: Send for Count Paris! Tell him the wedding will be tomorrow morning.

JULIET: I met Paris at the friar's. I showed my love for him.

CAPULET: I'm glad.

(to a servant): I need to see Paris. Bring him here. Our city owes Friar Lawrence. We should thank him.

JULIET: Nurse, will you help me in my room? I have to pick out my clothes for the wedding tomorrow.

LADY CAPULET: No, not until Thursday.

CAPULET: Nurse, go with her.

(to Lady Capulet): We'll have the wedding tomorrow.

*(**Juliet** and **Nurse** leave.)*

LADY CAPULET: We won't be ready!

CAPULET: Don't worry. All will be well. I promise you. Go help Juliet. I'll stay up tonight. I'll be the housewife this once.

*(**Lord** and **Lady Capulet** leave.)*

— Scene 3 —

(*Juliet* and *Nurse* enter Juliet's room.)

JULIET: Yes, those clothes are best. Nurse, will you leave me? I need to pray. You know I am a sinner.

(*Lady Capulet* enters.)

LADY CAPULET: Do you need my help?

JULIET: No, Mother. We're finished. Please leave me alone. I want to pray.

LADY CAPULET: Good night. Get some rest.

(*Lady Capulet* and *Nurse* leave.)

JULIET (*to herself*): We may never meet again. I am very scared. No one can help me.

(*She holds up a bottle.*)

What if it doesn't work? Will I be married tomorrow? No, this will stop it.

(She takes out a knife.)

What if this potion kills me? That would prevent the friar's shame for marrying me to Romeo. I don't think the friar would kill me. What if I wake up before Romeo comes for me? Will I die in the tomb? Come to me, Romeo. I drink this for you!

(She drinks from the bottle and falls on her bed.)

— Scene 4 —

*(**Lady Capulet** and **Nurse** enter a hall in Capulet's house.)*

LADY CAPULET: Get more spices.

NURSE: The bakers want more fruit.

*(**Capulet** enters.)*

CAPULET: Hurry up! It's three o'clock. Take care of the meats. Make sure there's plenty of food. Don't worry about the cost.

NURSE: Go to bed. Or you'll be sick tomorrow.

CAPULET: I'll be fine.

*(**Lady Capulet** and **Nurse** leave. **Servants** enter.)*

CAPULET: What have you got there?

FIRST SERVANT: Things for the cook.

CAPULET: Hurry! Hurry!

*(**Servants** leave.)*

> My goodness, it's day! I hear Paris. The band is coming. Nurse!

*(**Nurse** enters again.)*

> Go wake Juliet! Get her dressed! I'll go talk with Paris. Hurry!

*(**They** leave.)*

— Scene 5 —

*(**Nurse** enters Juliet's bedroom.)*

NURSE: Juliet! Wake up, sleepyhead. My, how soundly she sleeps. I have to wake her. Oh no! She's dead! I wish I had never been born! Help! Lord and Lady, come quickly!

*(**Lady Capulet** comes in.)*

LADY CAPULET: What's all this noise?

NURSE: Oh, sad day!

LADY CAPULET: What's the matter?

NURSE: Look!

LADY CAPULET: Oh my! My dear child, wake up! Or I will die with you! Help! Call for help!

*(**Capulet** enters.)*

CAPULET: Bring Juliet. Paris is waiting for her.

NURSE: She's dead!

CAPULET: What? Let me see her. Oh no! She's cold. Her joints are stiff. She's dead like a beautiful flower killed by frost.

NURSE: Oh, sad time!

*(**Friar Lawrence** and **Paris** enter.)*

FRIAR LAWRENCE: Is the bride ready to go to church?

CAPULET: She will go, but she'll never return. She is dead. Death has picked her like a flower. He has married my daughter. I want to die too. Everything dies!

PARIS: I was so excited for today. But now this happens.

LADY CAPULET: Oh, hateful day! Our only child is dead. She has been stolen!

NURSE: Oh, terrible day!

PARIS: Death has tricked me.

CAPULET: Why did this happen? I will never be happy again.

FRIAR LAWRENCE: Be still! She's in heaven now. Dry your tears. Dress her in her best clothes. Bring her to the church. She's gone to a happier place.

CAPULET: We prepared for her wedding. Now it will all be used for her funeral. Everything has changed.

FRIAR LAWRENCE: We will take her to her grave. The heavens are punishing you. Don't do anything more to go against heaven's will.

*(They **all** leave.)*

Act 5

— Scene 1 —

*(**Romeo** enters a street in Mantua.)*

ROMEO: I feel happy today. My dreams tell me good news is coming.

*(**Balthasar** enters.)*

Here is news from Verona! Hello, Balthasar! How is my Juliet? Nothing can be bad if she is well.

BALTHASAR: She is well. Nothing is bad. She's sleeping in the tomb. Her soul is in heaven. I'm sorry to bring you this news.

ROMEO: Is it true? I will leave here tonight!

BALTHASAR: Wait. You look pale. It wouldn't be good for you to leave like this.

ROMEO: No, you are wrong. Please help me get to Verona. I'll be right with you.

*(**Balthasar** leaves.)*

ROMEO: Juliet, I will lie with you tonight. How will I do it? I will go to the druggist. He's poor. He needs money. He'll help me. This should be the house.

*(knocking on the door)***:** Hello? Druggist!

*(**Druggist** enters.)*

DRUGGIST: Who is shouting for me?

ROMEO: Come here. I see that you are poor. Here are 40 gold coins. Please give me an ounce of poison. I need something that will kill quickly.

DRUGGIST: I have drugs like that. But the law won't let me sell them. I will be put to death if I do.

ROMEO: Are you afraid to die? You are very poor. You look very hungry. The law will not make you rich. Break the law. Take this gold.

DRUGGIST: I need the money. I'll do it.

(Druggist hands Romeo the poison.)

DRUGGIST: Mix this with liquid. Drink it. It will kill you right away.

ROMEO: Here is your gold. Money is a worse poison to men's souls. It does more evil in this world. Good-bye. Buy some food. Be well.

— Scene 2 —

*(**Friar John** enters Friar Lawrence's room.)*

FRIAR JOHN: Hello? Friar Lawrence?

*(**Friar Lawrence** enters.)*

FRIAR LAWRENCE: Welcome back. What did Romeo say? Did he write a letter for me?

FRIAR JOHN: I found another friar to go with me. He was visiting the sick. Health officials sealed the house. They thought it had been hit with the plague. We weren't allowed to go. I couldn't leave for Mantua.

FRIAR LAWRENCE: Who delivered my letter to Romeo?

FRIAR JOHN: Nobody. I couldn't send it. And I couldn't get it back to you.

Everyone was afraid of getting sick. Here it is.

FRIAR LAWRENCE: Oh no! This letter was very important. We may have caused much damage. Friar John, go and get me a crowbar! Bring it here to my room.

*(**Friar John** leaves.)*

FRIAR LAWRENCE: I must go to the tomb alone. Juliet will soon wake up. She will be angry with me. I promised I would get the letter to Romeo. I'll write to him again. I'll hide her in my room until Romeo comes. Poor girl!

*(**Friar Lawrence** leaves.)*

— Scene 3 —

*(**Paris** and his **servant** enter the churchyard near the Capulet tomb. The servant carries flowers and a torch.)*

PARIS: Give me the torch. Stand there. No, put it out. I don't want to be seen. Wait over there by those trees. Warn me if you hear someone coming. Give me the flowers. Go!

(Servant hides.)

PARIS: Sweet Juliet. I will bring flowers to you every night. I will water them with my tears.

(Servant whistles.)

Someone's coming! Who could it be? I will hide in the darkness.

*(Paris hides. **Romeo** enters with **Balthasar**. Balthasar carries a torch and tools.)*

ROMEO: Give me the ax and the crowbar. Take this letter to my father tomorrow. Give me the torch. Now go! If you peek at what I am doing, I will kill you. I am wild tonight. I am wilder than a hungry tiger!

BALTHASAR: I will leave, sir.

ROMEO: You have been a good friend. Be well. Good-bye.

BALTHASAR *(aside)*: I will hide nearby. I am afraid about what Romeo might do.

(He hides.)

ROMEO: You awful tomb. You have taken the woman I love. Open your jaws!

(He breaks open the door of the tomb.)

I will give you another body!

PARIS: That is Romeo. He murdered Juliet's cousin. Some say she died because of her

97

sadness. He has come here to harm the dead bodies. I will stop him.

(Paris comes out of hiding.)

Stop, evil Montague! I arrest you! Come with me. You must die.

ROMEO: I will die. That's why I came here. Don't try to stop me. Leave me alone. I came here to kill myself.

PARIS: That is crazy! I am arresting you. You are an outlaw here.

ROMEO: Do you want to fight? Let's fight!

(They fight. Paris's servant appears.)

SERVANT: Oh Lord! I will call the guards.

(Servant leaves.)

PARIS *(falling to the ground)*: You killed me! Have mercy on me. Open the tomb. Let me lie with Juliet.

(Paris dies.)

ROMEO: I promise. Let me see your face.

(He looks more closely at Paris.)

It's Paris! Mercutio's relative. He was supposed to marry Juliet. Isn't that what Balthasar said? Did I dream it?

(He takes Paris's hand.)

Oh, Paris! Both of us had bad luck. I'll bury you in this tomb with Juliet. Her beauty fills this tomb. You are buried by another dead man.

(Romeo lays Paris in the tomb, near Juliet.)

Oh, my love! You are still beautiful, even in death. Tybalt, I see you there in your bloody sheet. What can I do for you? I will kill myself, the man who killed you. Forgive me, cousin! Juliet, why are you still so beautiful? Death must be in love with you. He wants you for his bride. I fear that. So I'll stay here with you forever.

(He drinks the poison.)

Oh, honest druggist. Your drugs are quick. I die with a kiss.

*(Romeo kisses Juliet and dies. In the churchyard, **Friar Lawrence** enters. He has a lantern, a crowbar, and a shovel.)*

FRIAR LAWRENCE: I must hurry! Who's there?

BALTHASAR: A friend who knows you well.

FRIAR LAWRENCE: Bless you! Tell me, whose light is that? I see it in the Capulets' tomb.

BALTHASAR: My master, Romeo, is there.

FRIAR LAWRENCE: How long has he been there?

BALTHASAR: For half an hour.

FRIAR LAWRENCE: Go with me to the tomb.

BALTHASAR: I can't. He thinks I went home. Romeo said he would kill me if I stayed.

FRIAR LAWRENCE: Stay here, then. I'll go alone. I fear something bad has happened.

(going into the tomb): Romeo! Why are these bloody swords here? Romeo! You are pale! Paris too? Covered in blood? How awful! The lady moves.

JULIET *(waking up)*: Oh, Friar! Where is my husband? Where is Romeo?

(A noise is heard offstage.)

FRIAR LAWRENCE: I hear a noise. Let's leave this place! Your husband is dead.

Paris is dead too. Come, I'll hide you.
Someone is coming. Let's go!

(More noise is heard.)

I dare not stay any longer.

JULIET: Go! I will not leave.

*(**Friar Lawrence** leaves.)*

What is this cup in my love's hand?
Poison has killed him. Romeo! You
drank it all. You didn't leave any for me.
I will kiss your lips. Maybe some poison
remains there. It will kill me too.

(She kisses him.)

Your lips are warm!

FIRST GUARD *(offstage)*: Lead on. Which
way?

JULIET: Noise? I'll be quick. Oh, happy
knife!

(She takes Romeo's knife. She points it toward her heart.)

My body is your sheath. Let me die!

*(She stabs herself, falls on Romeo's body, and dies. **Guards** enter with **Paris's servant**.)*

FIRST GUARD: The ground is bloody here. Go! Catch anyone you can!

*(**Some** of the **guards** leave.)*

This is an awful sight! Paris is dead. Juliet is bleeding. She's still warm. But she was buried two days ago! Go, tell the Prince! Run to the Capulets! Wake up the Montagues!

*(**More guards** leave. **Other guards** enter with **Balthasar**.)*

SECOND GUARD: Here's Romeo's servant. We found him outside.

FIRST GUARD: Hold him for the Prince.

*(**More guards** enter with **Friar Lawrence**.)*

THIRD GUARD: Here is a friar. He looks troubled. We took these tools from him as he was leaving.

FIRST GUARD: How strange! Hold the friar too.

*(The **Prince**, **Lord** and **Lady Capulet**, and **servants** enter.)*

PRINCE: What's going on here?

FIRST GUARD: Paris lies here. Dead. Romeo is dead. Juliet is dead. She was buried before. But she's just been killed. She is still warm.

PRINCE: Find out how these murders happened!

FIRST GUARD: This friar and Romeo's

servant had tools with them. They may have opened the tombs.

CAPULET: Oh, wife! Our daughter bleeds! There is a Montague knife in her heart.

LADY CAPULET: Oh my! This is a warning of my own death.

*(**Montague** and **others** enter.)*

PRINCE: Come in, Montague. See your son.

MONTAGUE: My wife died last night. She was so sad that Romeo could not return to Verona. It killed her to think of it. What news could be worse?

PRINCE: Look. You will see.

MONTAGUE: Romeo! What bad manners! You should not have died before me!

PRINCE: Calm down. We must find out what happened.

FRIAR LAWRENCE: I can tell you what happened. Romeo and Juliet were married. I married them the day Tybalt died. Romeo had to leave Verona. Juliet was sad for Romeo, not Tybalt.

The Capulets planned her wedding to Paris. She came to me. She begged me to find a way to save her from this marriage to Paris. She said she would kill herself if I didn't help her. I gave her a sleeping potion. Everyone thought she was dead.

I wrote to Romeo and told him the whole story. He was to come for her. But Friar John could not deliver the letter. I came for her tonight. I found Paris and Romeo dead. Juliet woke up. I begged her to leave with me. I heard a noise. It scared me. She wouldn't leave. So I left the tomb. She killed herself. If you feel this is my fault, I am willing to die.

PRINCE: We still think of you as a holy

man. What does Romeo's servant say about all this?

BALTHASAR: I brought Romeo news of Juliet's death. He hurried here. He gave me a letter for his father. He said he would kill me if I didn't leave.

PRINCE: Give me the letter. I will look at it. Where is Paris's servant?

(to servant): Why was Paris here?

SERVANT: He came with flowers for Juliet. Someone came to open the tomb. Paris drew his sword on him. I ran away to call the guards.

PRINCE: This letter supports the friar's story. It tells of the love between Romeo and Juliet. Romeo found out about her death. He bought some poison. He came here to die with Juliet.

Capulet! Montague! See what your hate

has done. Heaven tried to stop your anger with love! I should have stopped this fighting. Everyone has been punished.

CAPULET: Montague, shake hands with me. Our gift to them will be an end to the fighting.

MONTAGUE: I'll raise a statue of Juliet in pure gold. It will honor her always.

CAPULET: And I'll do the same for Romeo. He'll lie beside her. They were killed by our hate.

PRINCE: This morning brings a sad peace. The sun will not come out today. Go! We'll talk more about this later. Some will be pardoned. Some will be punished. There was never a sadder story than that of Romeo and Juliet.

*(**All** leave.)*